For little ones everywhere

Little 1

by Ann & Paul Rand

Harcourt, Brace & World, Inc.
New York, New York

Little 1 looked like a stick.
From the front he was medium thick,
but from the side he was so thin
he could have been
a line.

Little 1 had very small feet
and a little red hat
that sat on the tip of his head.
He could hop and skip and spin,
but he never had much fun
because he was only 1.

"I'd like to be 2 like you,"
Little 1 said, smiling at 2 yellow pears
that lay in a dish.
"Go away," said the pears.
"2 is company,
but 2 plus 1 is 3,
and that would be
a crowd."

So Little 1 sadly set off
and right away met
3 stuffed bears lazing in the sun.
If 3 is a crowd, thought Little 1,
3 plus 1 is 4,
and that is even more.
So he didn't bother to ask
if he'd be allowed to bask beside them.

But when he began
to feel lonely again,
Little 1 asked 4 bees
who were building a hive
if he might give them a hand.
"5 can do more than 4," he said.
But the biggest bee
buzzed so angrily
that Little 1 scurried away.

Of 5 umbrellas standing in a rack
not one answered back
when Little 1 cried,
"May I climb inside?"
But when he said,
"I'm sure there's room for 6,"
a pink parasol sniffed,
"We've no room at all
for ordinary sticks."

Little 1 found 6 ants
searching for crumbs of bread,
but they were too busy
to pay any attention
when Little 1 happened to mention
that instead of 6
they could as well be 7.

7 mice playing hide and seek
with a cat
just brushed Little 1 aside
when he said,
"Wouldn't it be fun
to make 8 out of 7 plus 1?"

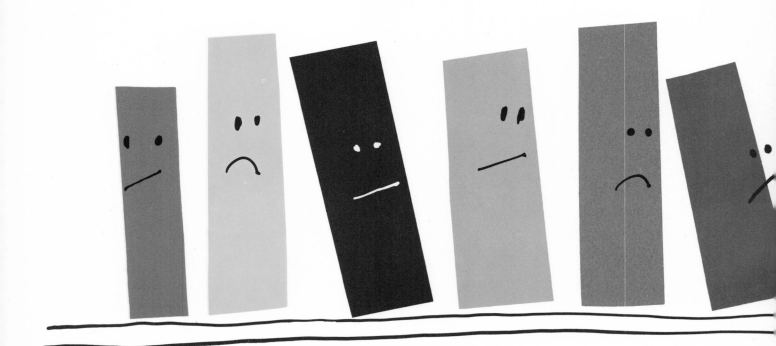

8 stiff-backed books
on a shelf
gave 8 cross looks
when Little 1 said,
"If I stand in line,
we could then be 9."

Little 1 was in such despair
he hardly dared
to stare into a big glass bowl
and tell 9 frisky fish
it was gayer when 10 could swish.
He felt no surprise
that each fish blew a bubble
and not one took the trouble
even to reply.

Little 1 felt very sad
and even somewhat mad.
"Whatever can be
the matter with me?" He sighed.
"2 turned away,
and none of the others wants to play.
Don't they know it's no fun
to only be 1?"

Little 1 was half ready to cry
when a bright red hoop
came looping by.
"Hi!" cried the hoop with a smile.
"Come and play for a while."
"But I'm only 1," said Little 1.

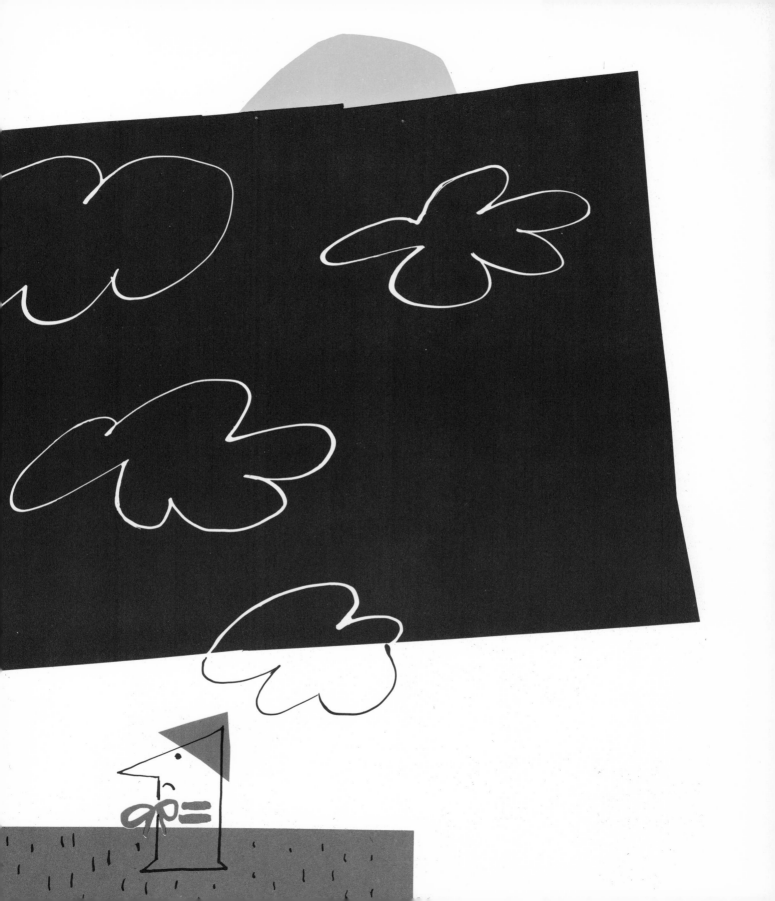

"Oh no,
that's not so," cried the hoop.
"Don't you know
a circle that's empty inside
is the same as zero?
Just stand here by me,
and then
you and I can be 10."

Little 1 and the hoop play together
in all kinds of places and weather.
When Little 1 pushes,
the red hoop swooshes away,
and Little 1 runs after
shouting with laughter.
Little 1 has found a friend
and has a lot of fun
now that he's no longer 1.

The End